First published in the UK in 2001 by

Belitha Press Ltd
London House, Great Eastern Wharf,
Parkgate Road, London SW11 4NQ

ISBN 1 84138 316 3

British Library Cataloguing in Publication Data for this book is available from the British Library.

Editor: Stephanie Turnbull
Series editor: Mary-Jane Wilkins
Designer: Sarah Goodwin
Illustrator: Liz Pyle

Printed in China

10 9 8 7 6 5 4 3 2 1

Contents

For Susan Austin
with much love - F.W.

For George and
Ned with love - L.P.

Gaoliang and the Dragon of Peking

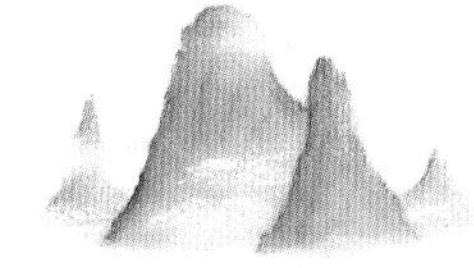

Many, many moons ago China was a land of dragons. These dragons were well-meaning and friendly as long as they were given due respect, but if crossed their rages were very awful indeed. No one would build so much as a chicken shed without consulting the local dragon. So when the Emperor Ming decided to design a great new city, to be called Peking, on the marshes of Youzhou, without so much as a mention or a by-your-leave to the resident dragon, he was asking for trouble.

Architects, builders and craftsmen came from all over China, for the emperor intended his city to be the most magnificent ever seen. There were carpenters and wood carvers. There were masons and painters. There were gardeners and tapestry weavers. Slowly the emperor's city took shape. Huge ornately-tiled towers rose into the sky. The streets were wide and elegant and fountains played in the courtyards. Jade carvings and painted wooden ceilings adorned the interiors. No expense was spared.

The dragon looked on all this activity and saw that a great part of his kingdom was being taken away. Anger rumbled deep in his heart and he resolved to teach the emperor a lesson.

One night, the emperor had a strange dream. He dreamt that an old peasant came to his palace, pushing two jars of water on a wooden cart. The old man asked the emperor for permission to take the jars out of the city and, seeing no reason to deny such a simple request, the emperor gave his consent. But the peasant was in reality the dragon in disguise.

As soon as he awoke in the morning, the emperor was greeted by the sound of wailing and crying from outside his window. All the wells and fountains in the city had dried up, for the jars on the cart in his dream had contained all the water in the city. There was not a single drop left.

The emperor was furious. He realized that a dragon must be behind this mischief and, although he knew that a dragon was a formidable opponent, he was determined not be beaten. He sent messengers through the city to check the gates. News soon came back that an old man had passed through the West Gate at dawn, pushing a heavily-laden cart towards the mountains. Now over the mountains and down the next valley lay the ocean and the emperor knew that if the dragon poured the water jars into the sea, Peking would never have flowing water again.

The emperor summoned his mighty army. Rank upon rank of heavily-armoured men stood in front of him, their great horses tossing their manes and

stamping their feet. The emperor recounted his dream and asked for a volunteer to pursue the dragon. The soldiers looked uncomfortable and shifted uneasily in their saddles. No one wanted to take on the anger of a vengeful dragon. But in their midst was a clear-eyed young man who loved his emperor, and he stepped forward. His name was Gaoliang. He flung himself flat on the ground in front of Emperor Ming.

'I will undertake this task for you, mighty Emperor. I will succeed or die in the attempt,' he declared boldly.

The emperor explained to Gaoliang what he had to do. He also gave him a long lance. When he caught up with the old man, Gaoliang was to pierce the water jars with the lance, without uttering a word. Then he should turn round and gallop as fast as the wildest wind back to the safety of the walls of the new city, without ever once looking behind him. Once the dragon realized what was happening, Gaoliang would be in mortal danger.

Gaoliang mounted his horse and soon all that was to be seen of him was a distant cloud of dust as he rode furiously in pursuit of the old man and the cart bearing the water supply. Gaoliang soon caught up.

Quick as lightning, he drew his lance and pierced a water jar. The water gushed out in a great torrent and nearly swept him off his feet. As he struggled to calm his horse before breaking the second jar, there was a mighty clap of thunder. Gaoliang saw to his terror that it wasn't an old man standing before him but a terrible dragon with eyes burning like coals and great scaly wings beating in anger.

Gaoliang turned and galloped for his life back towards Peking, the dragon's hot breath burning his back, the water gushing under his horse's hoofs. As he reached the city walls, in his great fear he forgot the emperor's orders and turned to see whether he had escaped the dragon. In an instant, a vast wave of water swept over him and he was drowned.

The dragon soared into the skies with a mighty roar as the emperor fell to his knees. Neither had really won, but both had lost. The water rolled on into the city so Peking had water once again, but only bitter well water. The jar that Gaoliang had failed to break contained sweet spring water and it remained where the cart came to rest. The place became known as the Hill of the Jade Springs and forever after whenever the citizens of Peking wanted to make tea, they had to walk outside the city walls.

The mighty dragon is remembered every year. On the fifteenth day of the first month of the lunar calendar, the people of China celebrate the end of Chinese New Year and the start of spring with celebrations including the dragon dance. Men dressed in black each hold a lantern on a stick, painted to look like a section of the dragon's body. They weave down the streets in a line so it looks as though the dragon is writhing along.

Jacob's Sukkah

JACOB WAS VERY OLD. His back was bent and his face deeply lined. He was always dressed in dusty black and his hands were gnarled and worn. Life had not always been kind to Jacob Leibman. He had outlived all his family, but he had many friends who loved him dearly, for Jacob was a generous man. He was not generous with money, for he had none, but he was generous with himself. He always had time to listen to the worries and cares of his friends and neighbours, and he shared their joys and sorrows.

Jacob lived in a small, simple house tucked away in the midst of a huge city. The other buildings towered over Jacob's lowly roof so that not much light and even less sun reached Jacob's rooms. Children would gather round his door after school and he would talk about the old days. While he explained how simple it had all been when he was a boy, there was always a twinkle in his eye as the children gasped at the thought of life without all their modern gadgets.

Jacob didn't own his little house, he was much too poor. The man who owned it and, more importantly, who owned the land on which it was built, was Thomas R Block. He was not a nice man. Jacob's neighbours didn't like him, as he was always bullying the old man. The children didn't like him, as he scowled fiercely at them and pushed them out of the way as he strode down the road. Even the cat disappeared like a wisp of smoke when he came near, as his boot had been known to stamp on a furry tail. A bitter and dreary man, Thomas R Block.

He was most bitter towards Jacob because as long as Jacob lived in his tiny house, Thomas R Block could not pull down the house and build a big mansion on the spot. Oh, how he longed to be rid of Jacob Leibman! He had great plans to become mayor of the city and live in a grand house. He thought it was all Jacob's fault that he didn't have enormous bags of gold coins to count every night.

He thought it was all Jacob's fault that the roof of the little house was always leaking, although the blame was his, for he paid so little towards repairs.

Jacob was a deeply religious man. He observed all the festivals that celebrate the history of his people, the Jews. At Chanukah he would light his special candlestick with the eight candles and place it in the window. He would give the children spinning tops to play with and chocolate money to eat. He spent days cleaning his house before Passover and then shared his unleavened bread and gefilte fish with as many friends as he could squeeze into his tiny parlour. And every year he would build a sukkah to mark the Jewish harvest festival, Sukkot.

The sukkah, a small hut built of branches and leaves, was a reminder of the time when the Jews had to seek shelter after their escape from Egypt. When Jacob was a boy his family were farmers living far outside the city walls and it was easy to find fallen branches to build the sukkah. Now it was much more difficult for him to find the materials in the city and he no longer had the strength to carry anything very far.

In the autumn of the year of our tale, Jacob started his preparations. He decided to build the sukkah on the flat roof of the shop behind his house. The children brought him branches from the one tired pine tree that stood in their dreary playground. Jacob saved some of his precious firewood. He walked slowly to the market and bought a few oranges and apples. One of his neighbours gave him some big vine leaves.

Carefully and painstakingly, Jacob carried everything on to the roof and began to build his sukkah. He made four walls with the firewood and laid the pine branches on top to form a roof. He wound the vine leaves through the branches and rested the apples and oranges on top. He carried a table and four chairs on to the roof and placed them under the leafy roof of the sukkah. It took him a long time and he was very tired when

he finally finished, but as he stood on his doorstep looking up at his sukkah, he gave a contented sigh and there was a smile in his eyes. It was well done. Now he could celebrate Sukkot properly.

The following morning, Jacob was woken by shouting and banging. As he rubbed the sleep from his eyes he realized that the commotion was coming from his front door. With trembling fingers he opened the door. There stood Thomas R Block, his face bright red with anger.

'Jacob Leibman! What is all that rubbish on the roof of my house?'

By now a small crowd of neighbours had gathered. They could see that Jacob was upset. He was wringing his hands and his face was white, his eyes full of sorrow. They began muttering and glaring at Thomas R Block. But he took no notice, for he saw that here at last was a chance to get rid of his sitting tenant. His grand mansion might yet become a reality.

'You will take that down by sunset or I shall see you are thrown out in the street. We can't have you making the place look untidy and anyway, it is against regulations!' and with that he stormed off.

The neighbours crowded round the distracted Jacob. Many were the offers of help and many hands supported him, but he shook his head sadly and shuffled back into his house, closing the door quietly. How could he now celebrate Sukkot? How would he be able to entertain his guests correctly if he had to remove his sukkah? He closed his eyes and prayed. When sunset came, Jacob had not moved from his chair and he had found no solution to the problem. A heavy pounding on the door told him that Thomas R Block had returned.

But when Jacob opened his door he found he was not alone. The whole street was filled with his friends and neighbours. Thomas R Block had been forced to fight his way through the crowds and they had not been gentle with him. But he was a big man and he was a ruthless man, and now that he saw his ambitions within his grasp, he would stop at nothing.

'Jacob Leibman, I have given you due warning. You have not removed all that rubbish of yours from my roof so now I am going to evict you from my house!' He moved forward to grasp Jacob by the arm and pull him out into the street. But Jacob's friends were not going to stand by and see him treated so roughly, and a nasty scuffle was about to break out when the voice of Rabbi Zukerman rose above the shouts.

In a loud, ringing voice he declared, 'Wait, Mr Thomas R Block! You cannot take the law into your own hands in this manner. If you think Jacob has a case to answer then you must go to the judge and leave him to decide.'

Well, of course, he was right and Thomas R Block had no alternative but to fight his way back through the crowds, who were even less gentle than before. He shook his fist at Jacob and shouted over his shoulder, 'Just you wait! I have right on my side!' and with that he disappeared round the corner of the street.

The next day found Jacob standing in front of the judge. He had never been in

a court before and he was very nervous. The gallery was filled with his friends, who booed when Thomas R Block walked in, but they were quickly brought to order by the clerk of the court. Jacob realized that only the judge could decide the events of the day. He had never felt more alone in all his life.

The judge asked Thomas R Block to state his case, and this he did with a great deal of pomposity, and more than a few untruths about what a good landlord he had been in allowing Jacob to stay in the house even though he was standing in the way of Thomas R Block's business interests. Jacob listened with a sinking heart. Put that way, he could see himself not only without his sukkah, but without a roof over his head before the day was done.

The judge turned to Jacob. 'Well, Mr Leibman, what do you have to say in answer to Mr Thomas R Block's accusations?'

Jacob stood up straight and looked directly at the judge. His face was calm, but his heart was beating so loudly he thought the entire courtroom must be able to hear it.

'Your Honour, Sukkot is an important festival for Jewish people. It is the time when we remember how our ancestors were forced to seek shelter in the desert after they escaped from slavery in Egypt. It is a rule of our faith that we build a sukkah, which must be in the open air under the sky, and I have always honoured this commandment. Sukkot begins tonight and lasts for seven days and seven nights, and I would ask that you let me abide by this rule of my faith.' Then Jacob sat down quietly.

The judge was wise beyond all telling. He understood that Jacob meant no harm. He understood how important it was to him to obey the commandments of his religion. He saw that Thomas R Block was mean and had no care for this old man who had lived his life quietly and simply without trouble. But he also saw that the city regulations were there to be upheld and, in a matter of law, Thomas R Block had right on his side. The sukkah would have to come down.

The judge wrote in the ledger that lay open on the desk before him, then he called Thomas R Block and Jacob to come and stand in front of the desk.

'It is against the law for anything to be built on the roof of a building. The sukkah must come down, or the full force of the law will be brought to bear against you, Jacob Leibman. Do you accept and understand my judgement?'

Jacob bowed his head, then looked up at the judge, his eyes brimming with tears.

'I accept and understand your judgement, Your Honour, and I will abide by it,' he said, bowing his head again. With a triumphant laugh, Thomas R Block turned to leave the courtroom, pushing aside the court officials in his way.

'Wait, Thomas R Block!' commanded the judge. 'I have not finished. The sukkah must come down, without fail,' and, turning to look once again at Jacob, he continued. 'The sukkah must come down. I give you, Jacob Leibman, exactly eight days to comply, and not a minute more!'

It took Jacob a moment to realize why everyone in the courtroom was cheering, and why Thomas R Block was looking like thunder as he once more turned to stride out of the court, which was now in complete uproar.

'Off you go, Jacob Leibman. Eight days and not a minute more!'

To this day, Jews construct shelters at home or in the synagogue to celebrate Sukkot. They eat, study or even sleep in them. During the daily services, sheaves of willow, palm and myrtle are waved and etrog, a type of citrus fruit, is carried round the synagogue, symbolizing God's presence at all four corners of the world.

CHILDE ROLAND

ONCE, MANY LEGENDS AGO, there was a Scottish king who had four children. Three were strong and fearless sons, and the fourth was a daughter who was as beautiful as the hawthorn in May, and she was called Burd Ellen. She had long, corn-coloured hair, skin as white as snow and lips as red as the rose in summer. She was as wild as the hills, her feet were always muddy and her petticoats torn, her hair tangled, and she was the despair of her mother, Fair Janet, the queen. Although Burd Ellen loved her two elder brothers, it was her youngest brother, Childe Roland, that she loved best.

On All Saints' Eve in late autumn, the four children were playing with a golden ball, trying to see who could throw it the furthest. Childe Roland threw the ball high in the air with all his might, so high that it blinded them as the sun caught its polished surface. No one saw exactly where it fell, but they knew that it landed in the churchyard.

With a toss of her corn-coloured hair and a swirl of skirts, Burd Ellen ran to find it before her brothers. No one noticed amid all the laughter that she ran widdershins round the church. Now widdershins is the way witches go, the opposite way to the sun, and Burd Ellen should have known better.

Time passed and she did not return. Her brothers called her name over and over again. They searched among the gravestones, but in vain. It was as if she had vanished into thin air. All the way back to the castle they expected her to appear suddenly, clasping the golden ball and teasing them for their slowness. The king was angry with them for not looking after their sister. As it grew dark, a gloom fell over the whole castle, for everyone loved Burd Ellen.

Days passed and there was no sign of Burd Ellen. Fair Janet grew pale and refused food, and the king feared he would lose his wife as well as his daughter.

In despair he decided he must resort to magic, as it was surely magic that had spirited Burd Ellen away. Saddling his great black horse, Roderic, he travelled many miles alone over the wild moors to seek out the old magician, Fionn. Few dared visit Fionn as he was known to be very powerful and in league with the faery folk, but the king was a desperate man.

Fionn was bent over a rough wooden table covered with ancient books of spells, mysterious jars and bottles of strange-coloured potions. Bunches of herbs and plants lay on the floor and the air was filled with a heavy, sweet scent. A fire burned low in the hearth, and a very large black cat with emerald green eyes looked unblinkingly at the king as he hesitated in the doorway.

'What brings the king to my humble hearth?' asked Fionn, turning slowly to look at his unexpected guest. His white hair tumbled over his shoulders and a great beard fell past his waist. His eyes were a piercing blue and surprisingly bright, gleaming out from beneath his bushy eyebrows. He wore a ragged purple cloak embroidered all over with gold and silver moons and stars.

Haltingly, the king told his tale. He told Fionn how much he loved his wild daughter and pleaded with him to help.

'So you want to match magic with magic, do you?' said Fionn, and his voice was angry. 'Never have you sought my help before, never have you honoured my learning before, but now you think I can conjure up a spell in an instant. Your daughter is in mortal danger, and it will take more than a few potions to bring her home safely.'

The king bowed his head in shame. He turned slowly towards the door.

'Wait!' commanded Fionn. 'I did not say I wouldn't help you. I will, but it will take great courage. Are you and your sons bold enough?'

'I do not lack courage on the battlefield when I can see my foes,' said the king, 'but I do not know how to face the unknown. I came to you because I have heard of your great skills and wisdom, and because I need your help. You will be rewarded as you wish, and richly, too, if you will only bring back my bonny Burd Ellen.'

'I do not seek reward, other than to see a smile on the face of Fair Janet once more,' said Fionn and he drew the king close to the fire. 'Now listen well, for if you do not heed my advice you will never see Burd Ellen again. She has been captured and imprisoned in the Dark Tower by the king of Elfland. He seeks to make her his queen and if you cannot rescue her before the ceremony on Midsummer's Eve then you have lost her forever. He has put an enchantment on her so she remembers nothing of her life with you and her brothers.'

The king felt a chill enclose his heart. He hated to think of his carefree daughter trapped and unable to see the light of day. The magician's voice broke into his thoughts.

'You must send your eldest son to rescue her. He must make his way to the land of Faery and climb the Green Hill. He must seek a way into the Dark Tower and there he will find Burd Ellen. She will offer him food and drink. He must not let one drop pass his lips or he too will be in the power of the king of Elfland forever. Go home now and give your son this quest, but remember – not one drop of food or drink!'

The king took a bag of gold from his belt and held it out to the magician.

'I don't need your gold, my king, and anyway you should wait until Burd Ellen is restored to you.' But the cat with the emerald green eyes was of a more practical nature and she took the bag from the king and hid it up the chimney.

The king galloped home through the night and told Fair Janet what the magician had said. But he missed out the part about needing to rescue Burd Ellen before Midsummer's Eve as he was sure that would only frighten her.

So the eldest son set out, with the magician's warning ringing in his ears. Long the king and queen waited, but he did not come back. When many moons had come and gone the second son came to the king and demanded that he be allowed to take up the quest, as his brother had obviously failed. Fair Janet said nothing but her cheeks grew paler still.

And so they waited again. The days passed and the long nights, and the year turned and still they waited. The second son did not return. The king began to look old before his time, for he knew that if Burd Ellen was not rescued before Midsummer's Eve she was lost forever.

At last one day the youngest son, Childe Roland, came to the king and Fair Janet and declared that it was now his turn to look for his sister. Fair Janet begged him not to go for he was her favourite and she could not bear to lose all her children, but he was resolute. With a heavy heart the king gave Childe Roland his blessing, repeated the magician's instructions, and gave him his grandfather's sword, the Sword of Sharpness.

'Your grandfather used to say that this sword was magic. Perhaps it will help you now,' said the king. And so Childe Roland set off on his quest.

He walked for days and days through mud and mire, over moor and through glen, under dark trees and over foaming rivers. He slept little and ate less, and he passed out of Middle Earth and into the land of Faery where all is not as it seems and magic whispers from every corner.

As he walked across a field of corn a huge white horse galloped up to him and whispered, 'Where are you going, Childe Roland, and what do you seek in the land of Faery?'

'I seek the Dark Tower where the king of Elfland has hidden my sister Burd Ellen,' Childe Roland replied, surprised to be talking to a horse.

'I know Burd Ellen. She is a friend to wild creatures,' replied the horse. 'You must follow this path for seven days and seven nights and then you will reach the Green Hill.'

Childe Roland thanked the horse and set off down the path. He walked for seven days and seven nights and, on the morning of the eighth day, came to the foot of the Green Hill. He was utterly weary, so he lay down on the grass to rest. On top of the Green Hill stood the Dark Tower. There seemed to be no way up the steep hill, and he could see no door or window that might let him into the tower. His heart sank, and for a moment his courage deserted him. How was he to rescue Burd Ellen?

'You must walk three times round the foot of the hill widdershins, Childe Roland, as the witches do, and the third time you must shout, "Green Hill, Green Hill, show me your path!"' said a quiet whispery voice by his head.

Childe Roland sat up and looked round. There sat a fine fox with a great plume of a tail. 'Burd Ellen is a friend to wild creatures,' said the fox and, with a single bound, he disappeared.

Childe Roland leapt to his feet and walked round the foot of the hill widdershins. As he circled for the third time, he shouted, 'Green Hill, Green Hill, show me your path!' and no sooner had the echo of his voice died away than a gleaming path appeared up the side of the hill.

Quickly he climbed the hill and soon reached the Dark Tower. The walls were smooth and thick and he could see no door in the dark stone. The wind blew chill and there was snow in the air. Childe Roland shivered, and not just from the cold. All his senses told him that he was very close to dark magic that he did not know how to defeat. Somewhere very near, inside the tower, lay Burd Ellen, bound by a powerful enchantment.

'Courage, Childe Roland! Do not despair, soon you will see your fair sister,' said a sweet voice in his ear. A little brown linnet sat on his shoulder, her feathers ruffled in the wind. 'You must walk once round the Dark Tower widdershins, and

once again as the sun goes and you must call out, "Open, Dark Tower, and let me in." Burd Ellen is a friend to wild creatures,' and with that she flew away.

Childe Roland did as she said and as he circled the tower for the second time and called out, 'Open, Dark Tower, and let me in,' a huge door swung open. Drawing the Sword of Sharpness, he stepped inside.

He was encased in velvety blackness. The only sound was his own breathing and the thump of his heart. The magical Sword of Sharpness gleamed faintly in his hand and, holding it before him like a torch, he walked slowly down a long passage. At last he came to two huge wooden doors which were half open. Cautiously he peered round and saw before him a vast empty hall, the roof so high that he could not see where it ended. The walls were bathed in a green light which picked out gold and silver lattice work covered in precious stones and draped with bundles of herbs. The floor was covered in beech leaves that whispered and rustled as Childe Roland stepped into the hall.

As his eyes grew used to the dim light he saw that a great wooden chair stood at the far end. There, in its dusty depths, sat his beloved Burd Ellen, slowly combing her golden hair with a silver comb.

With a cry of joy Childe Roland sprang forward and grasped his sister by the hand. But her hand was icy cold and when she turned to look at him, her eyes were lifeless. She was indeed under a deep enchantment. Then there was a crash behind him, and Childe Roland turned to see the king of Elfland in all his fury. He was dressed from head to toe in green. His long black hair lay braided down his back and he wore a golden crown. His eyes were green and glittering.

'So, Childe Roland, you seek to challenge me in my own kingdom!' he said, and his voice was like the hiss of a snake. 'You have come for your sister Burd Ellen, but I wish to make her my queen. We are to be wed tomorrow on Midsummer's Eve and then she will be mine forever. You cannot succeed where your foolish brothers have failed!' and the elf king drew back a heavy velvet curtain. There lay Burd Ellen's two brothers, cold and lifeless.

The elf king took Burd Ellen by the hand.

'Come, my dear. You have not offered your brother refreshment. He must celebrate with us.'

As he clapped his hands, the hall was suddenly filled with faery folk, laughing and chattering as they brought in bowls of wine and plates of sweetmeats. Burd Ellen took a golden goblet and filled it to the brim with ruby red wine.

'Drink this, Childe Roland. You look thirsty,' her sweet voice tempted him. But he dashed away the goblet as he remembered Fionn's warning. Burd Ellen then offered him food. His mouth watered and he almost took a bite. But when he looked in her eyes he saw the blankness and remembered again, just in time, Fionn's warning. He threw the plate across the room and it broke into hundreds of pieces.

The king of Elfland stood in front of Childe Roland and drew his sword.

'So, you ignore my welcome and challenge me, Childe Roland!' he spat. 'You will soon follow your brothers and Burd Ellen will be mine.'

He came at Childe Roland, sword raised in his hand. There was a loud clang as the two swords clashed and suddenly the air was filled with a great rushing wind. The elf king gave a cry of rage. His sword writhed in his hand and fell to the ground where it dissolved in a cloud of smoke. The Sword of Sharpness glittered in Childe Roland's hand.

'Who gave you that sword?' the king of Elfland muttered. 'It has a deep magic that is beyond my powers.'

'Undo the spells that bind my sister and my brothers or I will destroy you and all your kingdom!' cried Childe Roland.

The king of Elfland had no choice. He took a small bottle of purple liquid from inside his cloak and placed a few drops on Burd Ellen's lips. Straightaway her eyes blinked, the colour came back to her cheeks and she flung her arms round Childe Roland with a happy laugh. The king then gave some of the potion to her brothers and they too sprang to their feet, smiling and crying all at once.

No one noticed the king of Elfland slip away. The green light in the great hall faded as daylight poured in and a distant rumble was all that marked the falling down of the Dark Tower. Burd Ellen and her brothers found themselves breathing the clear air of the moors and felt the sun warm on their faces. And so they passed from that enchanted land and came home to the king and Fair Janet.

Burd Ellen remained as wild as the hills, but she was very careful never to go widdershins round a church ever again.

All Saints' Eve, or Halloween, is the last day of October. On this day the souls of the dead are supposed to rise up and visit their homes. The Ancient Celts used to call this time Samhain. Witches were said to roam that night and bonfires were lit to scare them away. The following day, All Souls' Day, has become a great Christian festival when prayers are said for the saints who don't have their own special day and for all the souls who have not yet reached Heaven.

THE COMING OF THE GREY ONES

IT WAS CHRISTMAS EVE. Pierre and Marie were standing outside the farmhouse, stamping their feet and flapping their arms, trying to keep warm. The sheep were milling about, sniffing the air anxiously as though they were reluctant to leave the warmth of their stable for fields where the frost lay white on the grass.

The children lived with their mother and father, Monsieur and Madame Duval, on a little farm in Brittany. They were poor as church mice and the farm was very tumbledown. They had three small fields where they grew cabbages and turnips, oats and rye. They had one old cow who gave them milk, several chickens and a small herd of sheep whose tangled fleeces Marie and her mother spun into wool to sell at the market. They all worked as long as there was light to see by, and although they had very little, they were a happy and contented family.

Every day Pierre and Marie would take the sheep into the meadows by the edge of the forest where the best grass grew, while their father worked in the fields and their mother fed the chickens, made butter and cheese and cleaned the house. She would pack a simple lunch of bread and cheese and perhaps an apple for the children, and every day as they left she would kiss them and tell them to take care.

In the spring and summer, it was pleasant to sit all day in the warm sunshine. Marie would spin wool while Pierre carved little wooden animals from holly and oak sticks. It was not so agreeable in the winter when the days were short and the cold wind blew and the snows began to fall. The children did not

mind the cold, as they could make a fire under the shelter of the trees, but they did dread one thing and that was fog.

It would creep up silently, rolling off the sea, blotting out all landmarks. The leaves of the trees would drip with moisture and on those days even the best fire could not keep out the chill. The children would strain their ears at every rustle and sound coming from the forest for their biggest fear of all was that the Grey Ones would creep out of the woods and surround them.

The Grey Ones were wolves. Great grey shaggy creatures, the wolves were strong enough and bold enough to snatch a sheep from the flock and slink away again into the murk. On foggy days, Madame Duval worried until the children returned in the evening, for what could a child do against the stealth of a wolf?

Madame came out of the farmhouse with their lunch in her hands.

'It is very cold today, children. See you wrap up warmly!' she said and, smiling, she gave them each a few chestnuts to roast on their fire as a Christmas Eve treat. Marie ran back indoors and brought out her red woollen shawl and Pierre's long scarf and then they set off, their breath making dragons' smoke in the crisp frosty air. The sheep followed the grassy path out into the meadow, nibbling the grass wherever the watery sun had melted the frost.

Once the sheep were grazing contentedly, Marie and Pierre looked at each other excitedly. They had a special plan. Because it was Christmas Eve, the children wanted to make a crib just like the wooden manger they had seen in the village church. It had carved angels and animals, and the little Christ Child with Mary his mother and Joseph his father. Marie was going to make the crib and Pierre had carved three wooden sheep specially.

Marie gathered some soft moss and armfuls of bracken while Pierre collected pine cones from under the dark trees at the edge of the forest. Marie filled the base of the hollow apple tree with the bracken and then lined it with the moss, and Pierre decorated the edges with the pine cones and some great trails of ivy, the dark green leaves still edged with silver frost. It looked beautiful.

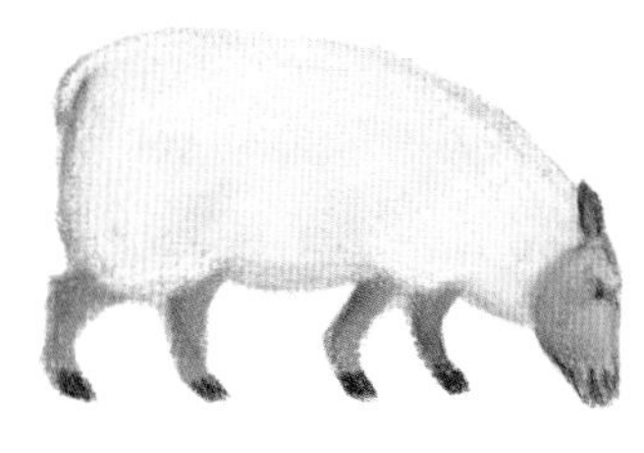

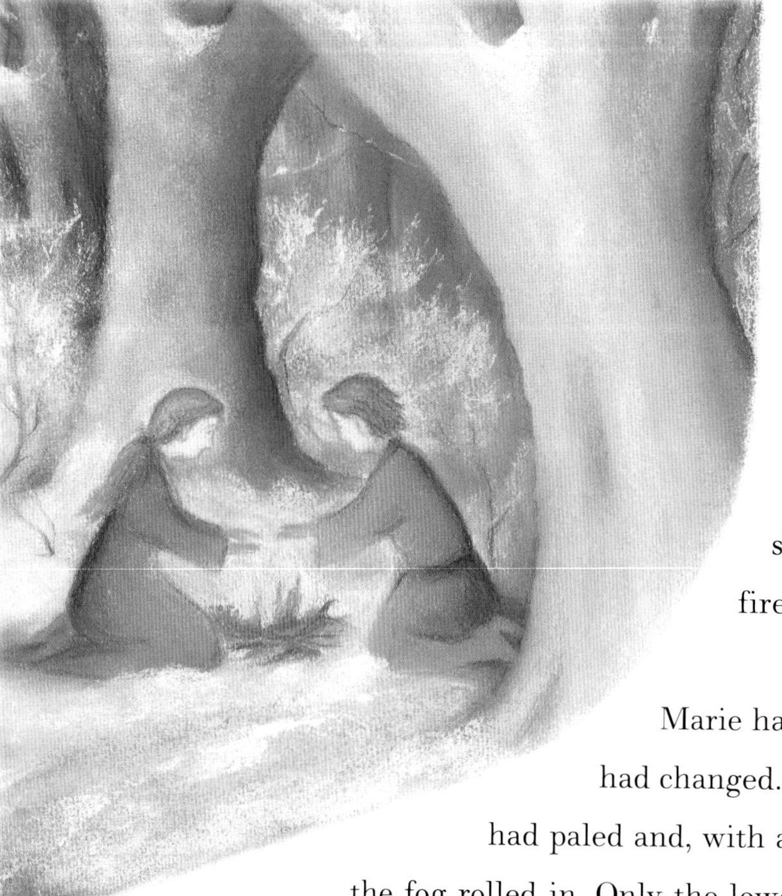

Pierre then lit a fire and when it was glowing at the heart he placed a flat stone on the edge and roasted the chestnuts. They were delicious and warmed the children's chilled fingers. The sheep gathered round the fire, huddled together.

But while Pierre and Marie had been busy the weather had changed. The low winter sunlight had paled and, with a sudden clammy breath, the fog rolled in. Only the lowest branches of the trees were visible and damp dripped off the leaves. The bushes looked like strange cloaked goblins. Droplets of fog clung to the children's hair and the damp seeped into their bones. They crept closer to the fire. The sheep were restless and looked around nervously. Everything was still. Not a sound was to be heard.

Suddenly the sheep scattered, bleating in panic, and before the children realized what was happening, three huge grey wolves came skulking out of the forest. Each wolf snatched a terrified sheep in its jaws. Then, as quickly as they had come, they disappeared into the trees.

Marie started to cry as Pierre frantically tried to calm the rest of the flock.

'Oh, Pierre! What will father say when we tell him we have lost three of our precious sheep? And what will happen to them, poor things?' sobbed Marie.

Pierre ran to her and they hugged each other in their fear. Another sound reached their ears. A rustling of leaves and a cracking of twigs. Pierre bravely snatched a burning branch from the fire in case it was the wolves returning, although he didn't know how he could defend his sister and the sheep if it was indeed the Grey Ones.

But it was not the Grey Ones. Walking slowly towards them was a small child, dressed all in white. His hair was a golden halo round his head. His face was pinched with cold and his tiny feet were bare on the frosty grass.

Marie ran to him.

'Oh, you poor thing! How cold you must be! Come and warm yourself by our fire,' and she took off her shawl and wrapped it round the child's shoulders. She led the child to the fire to warm his hands and feet, and then exclaimed, 'I know what would be best! Come and lie in our crib. It will shelter you and will be soft to lie on.'

The little child snuggled down in the crib with Marie's shawl and Pierre's big scarf round him like blankets. Pierre collected more wood and the fire soon blazed up, shedding a great warmth over the two children and the little one who now seemed to be asleep in the crib. Still the fog hung around them in a great heavy cloud and the mystery of the tiny child was forgotten as Pierre and Marie remembered their three lost sheep. The children knew their father would not be angry with them, for no one can fight wolves, and certainly not two children, but their loss would be grievous and on Christmas Eve too. So they sat huddled round the fire, their thoughts and hearts heavy, as the day slipped by.

Suddenly Pierre looked up in surprise. A shaft of sunlight appeared to be coming from the old apple tree.

But it was not sunlight. It came from the child who now stood by the crib, smiling, his hands outstretched towards the children.

Marie and Pierre took his little hands in wonder and the child led them away from the fire and into the forest. And they went with him, unafraid even though he was leading them under the gloomy trees, deeper into the forest where the wolves might be. He led them down a path they had never noticed before, through nettles and brambles which seemed to turn aside as the children walked by.

They came to a clearing and there stood a stable, a warm glow coming from inside. The doors were open and they all entered the humble building. There stood a manger, just like the one in church. Around the manger stood shepherds and, at their feet, the children recognized with delight their three lost sheep.

The little child turned and smiled at them, a smile of such intense sweetness that neither Pierre nor Marie forgot it for the rest of their lives. The child's golden hair dazzled them momentarily and when they opened their eyes again all had vanished – the stable, the shepherds, the manger and the tiny child. All except their three sheep who stood before them, safe and well.

The children ran back through the forest, down the path and out into the meadow again. There stood the rest of the flock, waiting patiently by the hollow apple tree. The fog had disappeared. Dusk had fallen and stars were twinkling in the clear sky. Marie and Pierre ran home with the sheep, back to where their mother and father were waiting anxiously. Words came tumbling out as the children tried to explain what had happened, the fog and the wolves and how the child had appeared to them. Their mother fell to her knees.

'That was surely the little Christ Child himself who guided you to our three lost sheep! He loves all sheep and shepherds, too. And now we must go to church to celebrate his birth all those thousands of years ago,' she said.

Pierre went whistling with his father towards the church down the street, their rough shoes ringing on the cobbles, but Marie showed her mother her red shawl. Wrapped carefully inside were the three carved wooden sheep from the woodland crib in the old apple tree.

To this day during Advent, Christian churches all over the world set up a crib to represent the stable where Jesus was born. The Coming of the Grey Ones *is based on a traditional Breton legend. The original concludes by saying that never again did wolves, the Grey Ones, plunder the Breton flocks of sheep on Christmas Eve.*

St George and the Dragon

The knight was utterly weary. He had ridden his horse hard through the day without rest and now they both needed food and a good sleep. Man and horse walked slowly through the city gates. The horse's head hung low, his sides were streaked with dirt and sweat, and he was limping slightly on one back leg. The knight's heavy armour was dull and his shield was so dented that the red cross on the surface was only just visible.

The knight was surprised by the silence that greeted them as the horse picked his way down the muddy street. Where were the townspeople? Normally the streets would be bustling, thronged with men, women and children, laughing and chattering as they went about their business. The silence was absolute.

Together the man and horse walked further along the street, looking to left and right as they went. A faint shaft of light fell on the ground. It came from the shuttered window of a tall but shabby building. The knight looked up and saw a sign, swinging gently in the night air. The building was an inn.

Thankfully, he led his tired horse through the courtyard to the stables at the back. There was no sign of a stable boy, so the knight rubbed down the horse with a handful of straw, filled a bucket with water from the well and thrust a generous handful of hay into the manger. Only when he was satisfied that the horse was eating contentedly did the man turn to look at his surroundings.

The whole place had a dilapidated air. Piles of dirty straw lay in one corner and a cart with only three wheels sagged in another. Empty barrels lay scattered by the back door and weeds were growing round the well in the centre. The knight walked to the door and struck it with his fist.

'Innkeeper! Here is a hungry traveller seeking a meal and a bed for the night. Are you open for business?' he cried.

Still the silence lay deep over the darkened courtyard. The knight struck the door with the flat of his sword. The sound rang round the deserted street.

'Innkeeper! Will you not open your door for a customer?'

At this there was the sound of a heavy wooden bar being lifted, then a tousled head peered cautiously round the door as it opened. It was the innkeeper, and he looked absolutely petrified.

'Who are you, and what do you want with us? We don't welcome strangers here,' he growled.

'I can see that for myself, good sir! Your entire city does not appear to welcome strangers. Never have I entered such a gloomy place. I am George of Cappadocia, a knight of the Red Cross, and I seek a quest. I was told your city might be in need of my services, but right now all I need is a hot meal and a bed for the night,' said the knight impatiently.

The innkeeper opened the door a little wider.

'A quest you say? Oh yes, we have a quest for you but I doubt it is one you will wish to undertake. It would be a bold man indeed who would take on the dragon,' and he laughed bitterly. 'You had better come in,' he said and opened the door, revealing a smoke-filled room with rough tables set round a huge open hearth where a great fire blazed. Several men sat at the tables, tankards of ale before them. All eyes turned to the knight as he strode over to the fire.

'This gentleman claims to be a great knight who will solve all our problems with the dragon,' shouted the innkeeper with scorn in his voice, and all at once a babble of talk broke out. The men looked at the knight as he stood warming his hands by the fire. He looked an unlikely saviour with his battered shield and dull armour, his cloak mud-splattered and his shoulders sagging with weariness.

'And what makes you think you will succeed where countless others have failed?' asked a young man boldly.

'I make no claims,' said the knight quietly, 'but I was told you were in need and I came, not knowing what the nature of your difficulty might be. The first I heard of a dragon was when your innkeeper here mentioned it.'

Everyone started speaking at once as they began to tell of the misfortune that beset the city. Only one old man, sitting in the corner smoking a long pipe, was silent, his eyes fixed on the figure bent over the fire.

The knight listened with growing irritation, until he could bear it no more.

'Be quiet, all of you!' he roared and there was an instant and total silence. The men looked anxiously over their shoulders at each other.

'Thank you,' said the knight. 'Now, first I need some food and drink and then, and only then, shall I listen to your tale of dragons, and then, and only then, shall I see what I can do to help you.' He was clearly a man used to being obeyed and the innkeeper drew a tankard of ale quickly and set it in front of the knight.

'As you see, sir, our terror has so infected us that we lose all sense of hospitality,' the innkeeper apologized. 'Of course you may eat and drink here and very welcome you are too. I shall see a bed is made up for you immediately in our best room and my wife will provide you with a plate of our finest stew right away.' Then he rushed out, shouting orders as he went. The knight drew long and deeply on the ale and stretched out his legs in front of the fire.

A low buzz of conversation began around him as everyone settled down again.

The stew was delicious and the knight had eaten two platefuls before he wiped his mouth and, sitting with his back against the warm stone of the chimney, surveyed the room full of anxious-looking men.

'So, you have a problem with a dragon?' he said, smiling encouragingly. 'Perhaps one of you might like to tell me all about it.'

The older man who had been sitting quietly smoking his pipe now stood up.

'My name, sir, is Richard. I am the watchman of this city and I am no longer proud to say that, for the name of our city has become associated only with this terrible dragon. No one knows where it came from, but it has besieged our walls for months now. It is a huge and terrible beast with great leathery wings and glittering scales on its breast. Its eyes are red as coal fire and its breath has such a stench that you would faint if you were downwind of its lair. Its mouth is cavernous and lined with rows and rows of iron teeth. It has a massive tail with a vicious spike at the end and deadly talons on its great feet.

'During the day this terrible creature slumbers in a vast cave outside the city gates, but as dusk falls it comes out roaring with hunger. Its fiery breath has scorched all the trees and fields of grain, and our crops are destroyed. At first it was content to steal our cows and sheep and pigs to satisfy its hunger, then it took even the cats and dogs, and soon there was not a living animal left.' Here Richard paused and looked round the room sadly.

'We were faced with a terrible decision. Should we offer ourselves to the dragon one by one and, if so, how should we choose who would be first? Or should we run the risk of the dragon destroying the entire city and everyone in it if it went on the rampage with hunger?'

'A terrible decision indeed,' said the knight, and as he looked round the room he saw that these were defeated and utterly terrified men.

'And so we decided to offer ourselves, one by one,' continued Richard sadly. 'Each day we draw lots, and the loser faces the dragon the next day at dusk. We fill a leather bag with diamonds and one red ruby. Each of us places a hand in the bag until someone draws out the ruby. That person becomes the dragon's next dinner. Every day someone has lost a loved one: a wife, a husband, a brother, a sister, a son, a daughter. Very soon we will all be dead. If you can help us, George of Cappadocia, we will fill your coffers with precious jewels and gold. They are all we have left, as the dragon cannot eat those.'

'I do not seek your jewels or your gold, but I will save you from this vile dragon,' vowed the knight, 'but first I must sleep.' He bowed to the men before turning and following the innkeeper upstairs to sink thankfully into bed, where he quickly fell into a deep sleep, untroubled by dreams, even of dragons.

The knight was up long before daybreak the next morning. He groomed his horse carefully so its white coat gleamed in the early morning light. He polished his breastplate till it shone like the rising sun peeping over the high walls of the city. The huge red cross on his shield gleamed. He brushed the mud out of his cloak and swung himself into the saddle. He rode down the main street towards the square where that day's victim would be selected. The crowd of people gasped with awe as George rode into the square. He looked magnificent.

Soon everyone left in the city was gathered in the square, even the king and his daughter the princess. Silence fell as the bag was passed from hand to hand, only to be broken with sighs of relief as person after person drew out diamonds. Then there was a gasp of horror as the ruby flashed red in the sunlight. It lay in the hand of the princess. With tears in his eyes the king stepped forward.

'We cannot let our princess die in this manner! We must draw again,' and he snatched the ruby from her hand. But the princess would have none of it.

'Father, I drew the ruby. I must share the fate of your people. I am not afraid,' and she stepped up to the knight on his shining white horse.

The knight lifted up the princess and placed her in front of him on the horse's great back, then together they rode out of the square, down the street and through the city gates. And so they waited as the day passed and the sun moved across the sky and the shadows lengthened. Every now and again a wisp of smoke drifted out of the dragon's cave and a low rumble shook the ground.

Gradually the rumbling became louder and then, with a blast of fire and smoke, the dragon heaved itself out of the cave. It was an awesome beast. It reared up on its monstrous feet, belching fire with every breath, its wings stretched out on either side of its scaly body. It glared at the figure of the knight, proudly astride his horse. The princess held her breath as the knight rode fearlessly close, keeping to one side to avoid the dragon's deadly breath. He brandished his long spear and its tip glittered in the red fiery light as he pointed it straight at the dragon's throat.

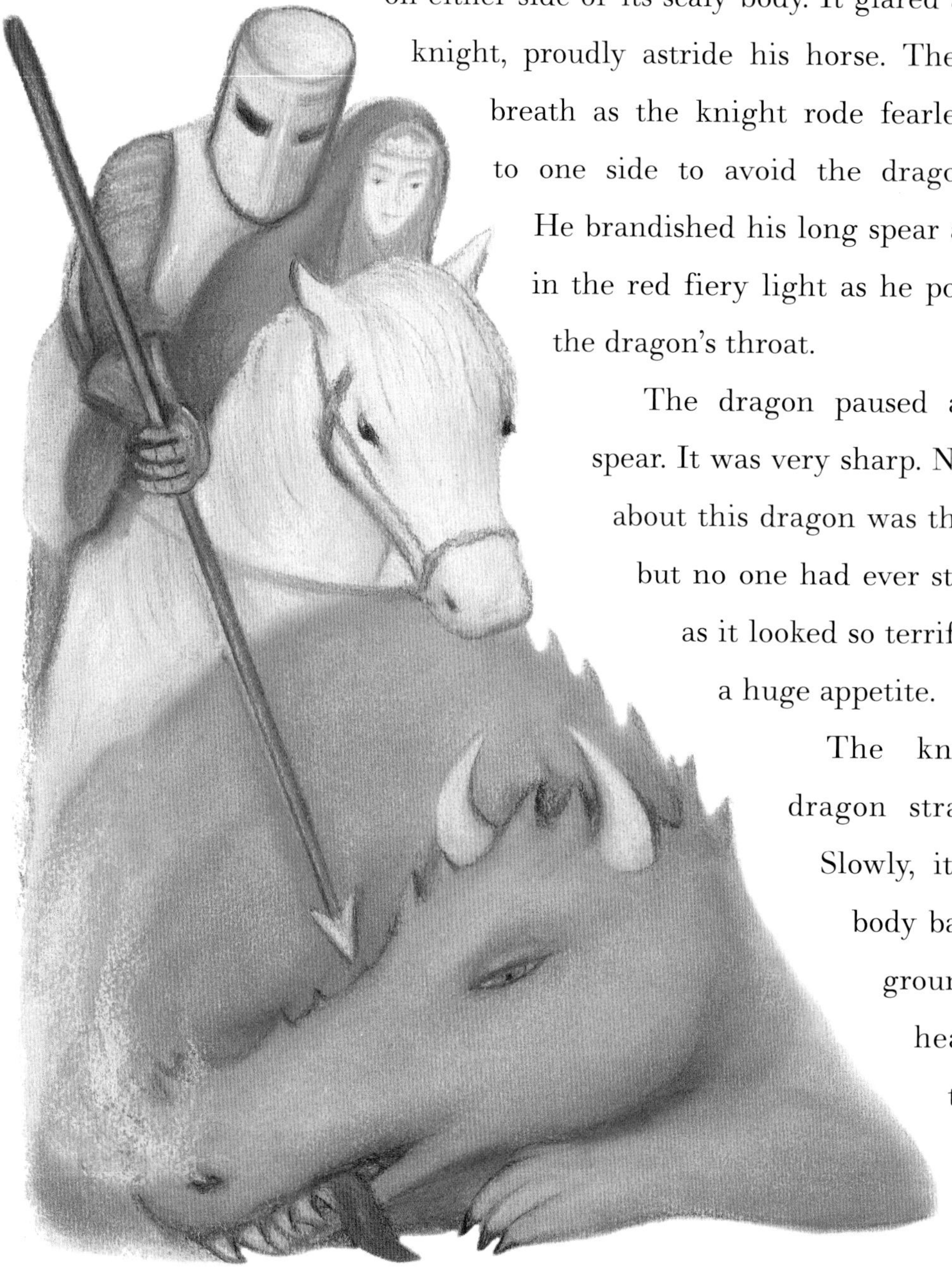

The dragon paused and looked at the spear. It was very sharp. Now the great secret about this dragon was that it was a coward, but no one had ever stood up to it before as it looked so terrifying, and had such a huge appetite.

The knight looked the dragon straight in the eye. Slowly, it lowered its huge body back down on to the ground and placed its head on its great taloned feet. One little spurt of fire puffed from its nostrils but then subsided again. The knight wound the sash from the princess' dress round the dragon's neck and slowly led it back to the city gates.

Richard the watchman had been standing high on the city walls looking out over the charred fields. He rubbed his eyes in amazement. Could it be true? He gave a great shout and rushed headlong down the steps and out into the square.

'My king, my king! George has tamed the dragon! The princess is saved!'

The king had been sitting with his head in his hands, tears slipping through his fingers, but when he heard Richard's cry he leapt to his feet and ran towards the gates. There indeed was his beloved daughter, smiling as she rode up on the knight's gleaming horse, George a little way behind her, the dragon meekly by his side. People ran hither and thither behind the king, no one quite daring to step out in case the dragon was only pretending. But it was indeed a changed beast. And ever after it protected the city, merely by its presence outside the gates. The farmers gave it food every day and, after a while, it quite lost its fierceness.

The king offered the knight the entire contents of the royal coffers, but George of Cappadocia declined it all.

'You will need your wealth to re-establish your city. Look to your fields and your meadows, your farmers and your herdsmen.' And he rode away in search of yet another quest, the setting sun glinting on his shining shield with its magnificent red cross.

St George's Day is celebrated in England every year on 23 April. There are many stories about St George and how he came to be the patron saint of England. We know very few facts about him, but it was Edward III who in 1348 founded the Order of the Garter, the highest order of knighthood, in his honour.

Prahlad and Holika's Fire

There was once a tribe of huge demons ruled by twin brothers called Hiranyaksha and Hiranyakashipu. This wicked tribe loved nothing more than descending to Earth and creating havoc. They plagued innocent people and animals and destroyed the crops farmers had planted. It is said that once they dragged the Earth into the sea and that was how the Great Flood came. Vishnu, the immortal and merciful god, saw what had happened and dived to the bottom of the ocean where he waged war against the brothers for possession of the Earth. After an epic battle that lasted more than a thousand years, Vishnu finally destroyed Hiranyaksha and brought the Earth back up out of the sea. From that point on, Hiranyakashipu swore revenge on the god Vishnu.

Hiranyakashipu consulted a seer to find out whether he would be victorious in his battle against Vishnu. The seer was blind, but as he took Hiranyakashipu's hands in his, Hiranyakashipu felt deeply uncomfortable, for it seemed to him as though the seer could see into his innermost thoughts. But the seer appeared to have only wondrously good things to predict.

'Great Hiranyakashipu, I can tell you that no man nor beast will kill you. There is no weapon forged that will kill you. You cannot be killed by day or night and you cannot be killed inside a house or outside.'

So it seemed to Hiranyakashipu that he was immortal, and he became very arrogant. His sister, Holika, was told by the same seer that she could never be destroyed by fire, and so brother and sister became even more wicked than before.

And then Hiranyakashipu's wife gave birth to a child. It was a boy and they called him Prahlad. As he grew up, it became clear that Prahlad was nothing like his father. He was a happy child, always smiling, and of a kind nature. He loved all the wild animals who would come to him in the woods without fear. Everyone loved him for his gentle ways, and it was whispered at the demon court that he would be a much better ruler than his father when he grew up. Of course these whispers eventually reached the ears of Hiranyakashipu, who became very angry.

'Prahlad will never rule, for it is prophesied that I cannot be killed by man nor beast, and so I shall never die,' he bellowed and ordered the guards to throw several of the courtiers into a deep pit, having first chopped off their ears for listening to gossip. He simply ignored his son, for he was not interested in anyone who was good and kind, and he had no wish to waste time on an heir who would never inherit. So Prahlad grew into a fine, tall and elegant young man, living a quiet life and avoiding the worst of his father's rule.

The burning hatred Hiranyakashipu felt towards Vishnu had not abated over the years, and he plotted to destroy the god. Imagine then Hiranyakashipu's rage when a rumour reached him that his own son was one of Vishnu's followers.

'No child of mine can worship Vishnu! Do you not know he destroyed your uncle, my dearest brother Hiranyaksha?' he screamed at his son.

'My beliefs cannot change, Father,' said Prahlad calmly but firmly. 'Vishnu is with us all the time and he guides our every action. He has come to Earth ten times to save us and it is his power that ensures good triumphs over evil.'

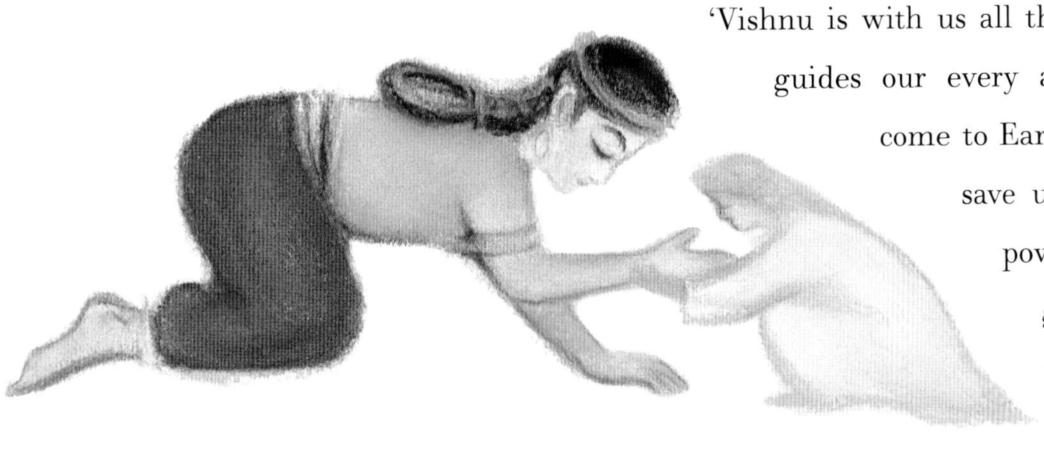

His face livid with anger, Hiranyakashipu ordered guards to seize Prahlad and throw him from the highest mountain in the land. No one wanted to obey this order, but they were all terrified of Hiranyakashipu. So they bound Prahlad hand and foot and put a blindfold over his eyes to lessen his fear, then carried him to the highest mountain in the Himalayas. The top of the mountain was lost in the clouds and it was a long, long way to the bottom. With many prayers for forgiveness, the guards pushed Prahlad over the edge and scrambled back down to report that the deed was done. But who should they see but Prahlad walking towards them, completely unharmed.

Hiranyakashipu was incandescent with fury and even more so, if that were possible, when Prahlad said,

'You see, Father, Vishnu is able to be everywhere at once. He caught me safely in his arms and brought me gently down to Earth.'

'Guards! I want you to build me the greatest bonfire there has ever been, and when the flames reach the sky you will toss this wicked boy into the very heart of the pyre!' roared Hiranyakashipu.

The bonfire was prepared. Huge logs were piled higher than the temple walls and everyone thought that Prahlad's last hour had come. Hiranyakashipu summoned his wicked sister, Holika, and bid her carry the tightly-bound Prahlad deep into the fire.

'I do not want this brat of mine to escape a second time, sister. As you can never be destroyed by fire, I want you to hold him in the flames until he is dead. Then everyone will see that my power is unchallenged and that I am the greatest god there has ever been and will ever be.'

The bonfire was lit and as the flames rose higher and higher into the sky, Holika slung Prahlad over her shoulder and strode deep into the heart of the blaze. Everyone gasped, for surely no one could escape the intense heat of the fire. Hiranyakashipu smiled an evil smile and strode back to his palace. He knew it would be some time before Holika walked out with the dead Prahlad.

The fire burned on and on, the heat never abating, the flames still shooting high into the darkening sky as the sun set. Hiranyakashipu was sipping a cool glass of tea when a flustered courtier was pushed into the room, bowing so low that his nose nearly touched the floor.

Hiranyakashipu frowned at the courtier.

'Well? Have you come to tell me that Prahlad is finally dead, eh? Speak up, man. I can't hear what you are muttering down there,' he scowled.

'The fire is no longer burning, my lord.'

'Yes, yes! And Holika…?'

'Holika has not come out of the fire, my lord.'

'WHAT?' roared Hiranyakashipu.

'A-n-d, a-n-d…' stuttered the petrified courtier.

'And what?' thundered Hiranyakashipu.

'Prahlad is still alive,' and so saying the courtier turned and fled, not wishing to have his tongue or, even worse, his head removed in Hiranyakashipu's rage.

Holika was still engulfed in flames, but Prahlad stood unscathed among the ashes. He bowed politely to his father, then stood up straight and said in ringing tones,

'Once more I have been saved by the grace of the great Vishnu!'

This was more than Hiranyakashipu could bear and, drawing his sword, he rushed at Prahlad, madness in his eyes. Suddenly there was a mighty clap of thunder and in front of Hiranyakashipu stood a strange beast.

The head and shoulders were those of a huge lion, the rest of the body was human. The creature picked up Hiranyakashipu as though he weighed no more than a bag of feathers and carried him to the great arched entrance of the palace.

Just as the sun sank over the horizon and dusk fell, the creature raked his fearsome paws across Hiranyakashipu's face and he fell dead at its feet. With another clap of thunder, the creature revealed itself as none other than Vishnu. The god lifted up Prahlad and, embracing him, said,

'Brave Prahlad, your faith has saved you. Now rule your people with wisdom and honesty. When your allotted time is done I will greet you in paradise where you will find eternal rest,' and with that Vishnu was gone.

So the seer's prophesy was fulfilled, though not in the way Hiranyakashipu had interpreted it. Vishnu appeared as half-man, half-beast. He killed Hiranyakashipu with a lion's claws, not a weapon. They were standing on the threshold of the palace so were neither inside nor outside, and dusk was falling, so it was neither day nor night. And as for Holika, she is still burning!

Holi, the Festival of Fire, is celebrated by Hindus every year as the wheat harvest is gathered in. Great bonfires are built, with images of Holika and a large branch in the middle to represent Prahlad. As the fire burns, the images of Holika are destroyed but the branch is pulled out to symbolize Prahlad's miraculous survival. People also throw powder and coloured water over each other in remembrance of the god Krishna, who loved playing such tricks on his friends.

The First Thanksgiving

SQUANTO PULLED HIS BLANKET round his neck and huddled into its warmth. The wind howled and the rain lashed against the roof of his hut. It was December, and winter had a fierce grip on the land. All day Squanto had watched a ship riding wildly at anchor in the bay of Plymouth Harbour. He could see the ship was in danger of sinking. He could also see that it was English and, as he had no love for pale-faced Europeans, he had returned to his shelter in the woods.

Many years before, Squanto had watched a similar ship arrive in Plymouth Harbour. He had been a young man, one of the Pawtuxet people who were originally a tribe of Wampanoag, The People of the Dawn. The Pawtuxets were farmers and fishermen. Food was plentiful and every autumn they gave thanks to Mother Earth at a special festival called the Green Corn Dance.

But one spring morning, a tall sailing ship appeared in Plymouth Harbour, its decks lined with Englishmen. White men had been visiting the shores more and more, capturing men for slaves and killing all who resisted. They had no respect for the land, and left disease and destruction wherever they went. Squanto and his people watched as the clumsy white men waded ashore and lit a fire. One of them approached the Pawtuxets and invited them to share his food.

Warily, Squanto and his companions sat with the Englishmen round the fire. The white men seemed to want furs and barrels of salted fish. When they invited a group of the young men, including Squanto, to board the ship to look around they had gone willingly. But it had been a trick. No sooner were Squanto and his companions on board than they were seized and flung into the hold, their wrists and feet thrust into manacles. The ship started to move and Squanto realized with horror that he had been captured as a slave.

The men were roughly treated by the sailors, and they were given only hard biscuits and dirty water to drink. Squanto missed the wind on his face and the warmth of the sun, but most of all he missed the peace of the forest. The ship creaked and groaned as it rode the waves and Squanto lost all sense of direction and time as he lay in the filthy hold. Some of the Pawtuxet men grew sick and they all feared for their lives.

When they reached land, the Pawtuxets were herded on to the deck. They were prodded and poked like cattle by richly-dressed men. Squanto looked around in great curiosity. The land was very different from Plymouth Harbour. Although he did not know it, Squanto had landed in Spain. Then followed a bleak and confusing time. He was sold to an Englishman and shipped to London.

After several years of slavery in England, Squanto finally gained his freedom. In 1619 he boarded a ship to go home, happy beyond belief that he was to be reunited with his people. But when he landed at Plymouth Harbour he found the village deserted, the fields overgrown with weeds, and not a living soul remaining. One of the English ships had brought the plague to his country and all his people were dead. In his grief Squanto wandered aimlessly for months, living off berries and fruits in the forest until the following spring when he joined Massasoit, Chief of another tribe of the Wampanoag.

And now Squanto feared disaster again. At dawn he rose and put on his buckskin jacket and moccasins. He moved silently through the forest and, hidden from view, looked out to sea. A boat was struggling through the waves towards the shore. The men inside were hunched over the oars as they pulled deeply in the final lap to the beach. Squanto looked further out to sea. The ship was still there. Squanto could just make out its name: *Mayflower*.

The boat landed and, as Squanto watched, the men lit a fire in the deserted village and warmed themselves. Then they fell to their knees and prayed and sang hymns to their god. The Pilgrim Fathers had arrived in the New World. Squanto returned home to tell Massasoit what he had seen.

'A ship is anchored in the harbour and several men have come ashore. They are white men,' said Squanto, his voice heavy with anger. 'I do not trust them.'

'Observe the invaders but keep yourself unseen. We shall see what their intentions are before we reveal ourselves,' said Massasoit quietly. He understood Squanto's anger and distrust, but he was a wise man who never acted hastily.

The Pilgrims decided to make a settlement at Plymouth Harbour. In the freezing snow and icy wind they felled trees and began to build wooden homes. Squanto watched as they worked, slowly and without skill, and he listened as they prayed and sang their hymns. He saw that these men knew nothing about farming or hunting. Gradually their food ran out and the Pilgrims started to become ill.

And then they began to die. In January eight graves were dug. In February there were seventeen. In March thirteen new graves appeared.

The *Mayflower* set sail once again, leaving only fifty-seven Pilgrims still alive, but not one of them gave up their harsh way of life to return to England.

Squanto, despite himself, admired their perseverance, if not their abilities. They had planted unsuitable crops such as wheat and barley. They had killed a few wildfowl and found mussels and clams, but they were thin and close to starvation.

'These are brave men, if foolish,' he said to Massasoit one evening. 'I do not think they will survive another winter without help.'

The next morning, Massasoit sent a messenger to the English settlement. The Pilgrims were astonished to see a tall and dignified Native American, clad only in a loincloth, stride into their midst.

Now the Pawtuxets had reason enough to fear the Englishmen who had ruined their land, but the Englishmen in their turn were very afraid of the Native Americans, whom they saw as terrible savages. The men reached for their guns in alarm, but the Native American raised his hands in a gesture of peace and greeted the astounded Pilgrims in English.

'You are welcome, Englishmen. I come to offer you help.'

The Pilgrims were amazed that the messenger spoke English, and they responded with cautious enthusiasm. After some discussion, the Native American returned to Massasoit with the news that the white men seemed friendly. Massasoit called to Squanto and together they approached the Pilgrims, carrying baskets of food.

The Pilgrims told Squanto of the persecution they had endured in England which had driven them to seek out a new life far from home. And he understood that they were men of great courage with a deep faith in their god, and he saw that they could work together. When Massasoit left Plymouth Harbour the following morning, Squanto stayed behind with the Pilgrims. He had finally come home to his village.

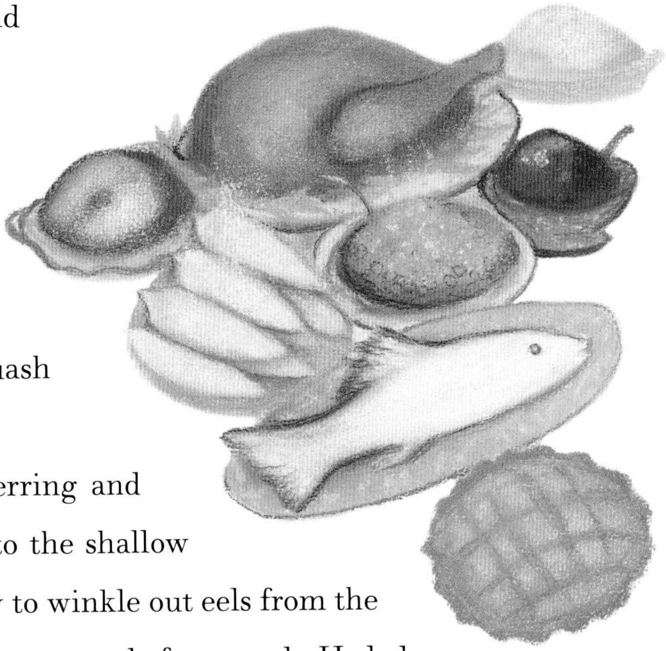

Squanto was wise in all things wild and he taught the Pilgrims how to survive. He showed them how to grow Indian corn. He taught them to plant beans alongside the corn so that the beans were supported by the corn stalks. He showed them how to grow squash and pumpkins between the rows.

He showed them how to catch herring and where the salmon ran. He led them into the shallow water of the river and showed them how to winkle out eels from the mud. He explained how to set the lobster pots made from reeds. He led them into the forests and showed them where to find wild turkeys and deer. He taught them which wild berries and nuts and seeds were good to eat. And all the time he tried to pass on to them his own love and respect for the earth.

That year, 1621, the harvest was plentiful beyond belief. Barns were full to the roof with corn and beans. Dried fish and meat filled barrel after barrel. Berries and nuts were piled high. Everyone had more than enough to eat.

In gratitude, the Pilgrims invited Massasoit and his people to join them for a harvest supper. The women were baking and cooking for days. Great tables were laid down the main street in Plymouth and roast turkeys and huge platters of vegetables were set out. The celebrations lasted three days. The Pilgrims saw it as a harvest festival, the Indians as a Green Corn Dance. It was both and so this joint celebration was the first Thanksgiving.

In 1864, President Abraham Lincoln ruled that the fourth Thursday in November should be a national holiday to remember that first Thanksgiving in 1621. It is a great occasion for American families all over the world. Traditionally they eat turkey and pumpkin pie.